For Calin, Akash, and Lilla
For Sang-Mi

*

And for Michiko, who lives by the river–G.O.

*

For Niklas and Lukas–L.W.

"A complete listing of the raccoon's foods would be
long, tedious, and perhaps impossible."
–Samuel I. Zeveloff, *Raccoons: A Natural History*

Text copyright © 2019 by Griffin Ondaatje.
Illustrations copyright © 2019 by Linda Wolfsgruber.
First published in Switzerland under the title *Der Tellerdieb*.
English text copyright © 2019 by NorthSouth Books, Inc., New York 10016.

First published in the United States, Great Britain, Canada, Australia, and
New Zealand in 2019 by NorthSouth Books, Inc., an imprint of NordSüd Verlag AG,
CH-8050 Zürich, Switzerland.

Distributed in the United States by NorthSouth Books, Inc., New York 10016.
Library of Congress Cataloging-in-Publication Data is available.
ISBN: 978-0-7358-4337-0 (trade edition)
1 3 5 7 9 – 10 8 6 4 2
Printed in Latvia by Livonia Print, Riga, 2019.
www.northsouth.com

Griffin Ondaatje

Linda Wolfsgruber

Muddy

The Raccoon
Who Stole Dishes

North
South

Out of the city where the highway ends and the road turns to gravel and the gravel turns to dirt and grass begins to grow by Mud River ... lived a raccoon.

Like all raccoons, he knew how to take care of himself. He ate at night and slept at the top of a tree all day.

His name was Muddy Whiskers, and he still lived with his parents.

Muddy was ordinary. He weighed fifteen pounds, was ten inches tall, and could open most garbage lids in under a minute. But he couldn't stand ordinary raccoon food. He refused to eat frogs, slugs, acorns, turtle eggs, crayfish, or clams. He only wanted to eat garbage–any leftover food he could find–and he liked to eat it on plates.

"Our son's a picky eater," his parents would say.

His parents–Mr. and Mrs. Whiskers–were hardworking raccoons. Every night they stood on the shore of Mud River with other raccoons, digging for clams. They dunked each clam in the water–seventeen times–as raccoons do. And, after eating, they washed the shells and left them in big piles on the riverbank.

Then they stood and gazed at a fancy new restaurant across the river.

All of the Mud River raccoons used to live in the city. And all of them were banished because they'd eaten too much garbage.

None of them wanted to get in trouble again–so every raccoon promised not to cross Mud River to steal people's leftovers.

Muddy was the only raccoon who couldn't make that promise. "Why shouldn't we eat delicious leftovers if they leave them in big bins for us to find?" he asked his parents. So he stayed in his tree and kept thinking about garbage.

Each evening his father stood at the bottom of the tree and
called to Muddy:

"Why don't you come down here . . . and help us wash these
clams!"

"I'm busy," Muddy called down.

But Muddy was only busy waiting for the restaurant to open.

When the Open sign flashed on, Muddy hurried across the river–to Le Grand Bistro–stole a plate from the patio, then dug through the garbage bins, piling on whatever he could find. He'd eat, then dunk the plate–seventeen times–and add it to a big pile on the riverbank.

Muddy's parents were worried–knowing Muddy was somewhere eating garbage.

"He'll cause trouble," Muddy's father muttered.

And sure enough, one night, Muddy did. . . .

Muddy left his tree, ready to eat soggy pizza, dry corncobs, and sticky marshmallows.

But when he got across the river, Muddy noticed the door to the restaurant kitchen was open. He looked inside and saw a big plate full of golden French fries.

Muddy climbed up onto the counter, took a French fry and dipped it seventeen times in a glass of water, and ate as fast as he could.

This is easier than looking for leftovers, he thought.

Suddenly he heard footsteps . . .

He grabbed the plate and floated it on the water, nudging
it across with his nose. As Muddy climbed out of the water,
he bumped into his parents.

His father's eyes widened. "Where did you get that plate?"

"From the restaurant across the river!" Muddy said,
dropping the plate and spilling the fries.

His father's short hairy arms poked the air, and his paws
frantically pulled his ears. "Raccoons don't steal plates!"
he cried. "What were you thinking?"

"Calm down," Muddy's mother said. "You'll attract
the other raccoons."

His father stroked his ears till he calmed down.

But by now a crowd of raccoons had gathered.

"I thought we'd agreed not to steal leftovers!" an old raccoon said. "Now your son's stealing plates?"

"Our son's a picky eater," said Mrs. Whiskers, wringing her paws.

"That's no excuse!" insisted the old raccoon. "He'll get us all in trouble!"

The wise, old raccoon had been chased out of more garbage bins than anyone. His nose was scratched, and the tip of his tail was missing.

"How many plates have you stolen, Muddy?" he asked.

"A lot." Muddy showed his parents and all the other raccoons the gleaming plates stacked in piles down shore.

Amazed, the old raccoon said, "Well . . . we'll have to wash the plates again and return them to the restaurant."

"Good idea!" agreed Muddy's parents. "And Muddy will promise not to steal leftovers again!"

The raccoons formed a line along the shore—each dipping a plate seventeen times. They washed and scrubbed the plates with their sensitive fingers until they sparkled.

Then the old raccoon said, "Lead the way to the restaurant, Muddy."

Muddy and all the others waded across the river, all of them holding plates above their heads.

When they reached Le Grand Bistro, Muddy hurried to the head waiter and held up the plate. "I stole your plates," he said (in raccoon language). "We washed them, so you don't have to wash them again!" His mother nudged him forward.

"And as I stand here before you I promise with all my heart to stop eating your leftovers."

But by then every person had left the restaurant.

Muddy stood up and eyed all the plates.
"Well, it seems a waste not to eat all this food!"

ACKNOWLEDGMENTS

I'd like to thank my youngest child, whose love of cupcakes partly inspired this story.

Raccoons handle food expertly–the way a jeweler handles gemstones–and they don't waste it. Something about the way they show up across the world, to find leftovers, ensures we won't forget nature. They might be the environment's smallest and funniest activists.

Love and thanks always to Sang-Mi.

I'd like to thank Linda Wolfsgruber for creating a genuinely beautiful world for the community of raccoons. I'm very grateful to Katja Alves, who believed in the story, and to Herwig Bitsche and everyone at NordSüd Verlag. Many thanks to my editor, Beth Terrill, and NorthSouth Books. Thanks to Patsy Aldana. Thanks to Lilla, Calin, and Akash. And to Sun-Mi, Simon, Craig, Darren, and Antony. Thanks and love to Mom and Dad. Thank you, Michiko, for everything.

–G.O.
May 2018